W9-DBG-839

U.S.A. TRAVEL GUIDES

OREGON

BY ANN HEINRICHS • ILLUSTRATED BY MATT KANIA

The Child's World®
childsworld.com

Published by The Child's World®
1980 Lookout Drive • Mankato, MN 56003-1705
800-599-READ • www.childsworld.com

Printing
Printed in the United States of America
PA02334

Ann Heinrichs is the author of more than 100 books for children and young adults. She has also enjoyed successful careers as a children's book editor and an advertising copywriter. Ann grew up in Fort Smith, Arkansas, and lives in Chicago, Illinois.

About the Author
Ann Heinrichs

Matt Kania loves maps and, as a kid, dreamed of making them. In school he studied geography and cartography, and today he makes maps for a living. Matt's favorite thing about drawing maps is learning about the places they represent. Many of the maps he has created can be found in books, magazines, videos, Web sites, and public places.

About the
Map Illustrator
Matt Kania

*On the cover: Take in the beautiful views of the
Pacific Northwest when you visit Oregon.*

OUR OREGON TRIP

Hey! Are you up for a trip through Oregon? You'll have so many adventures there! You'll raft down a rushing river. You'll swim in a volcano. You'll hunt for **fossils** and sparkly rocks. You'll see how cheese and blankets are made. You'll meet sea lions and wild horses. You'll gaze at distant stars. And you'll watch salmon leap uphill!

Are you ready? Then let's not wait. Just buckle up and hang on tight. We're off to see Oregon!

WELCOME TO OREGON

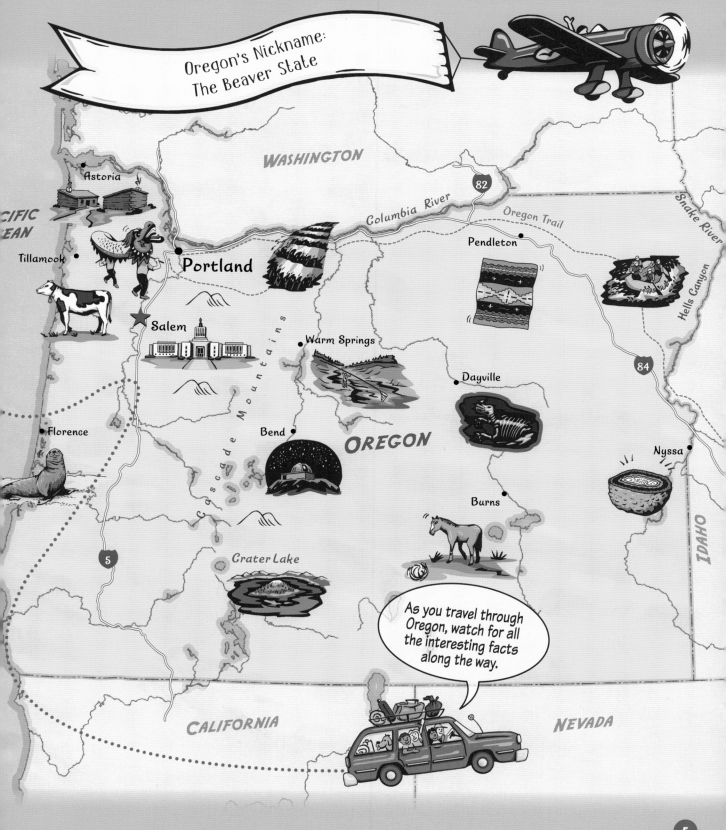

CRATER LAKE IN THE CASCADE MOUNTAINS

Want to swim in a volcano? Then jump into Crater Lake. It's a volcanic crater called a caldera!

Crater Lake is in the Cascade Mountains. These snowcapped peaks are Oregon's biggest mountain range. They tower over meadows, forests, and swift streams.

The Columbia River flows through the Willamette Valley and the Cascades. Finally, it flows into the Pacific Ocean. Oregon's western border faces the ocean.

The Willamette River runs through western Oregon. The area is known for its fertile farmland. Central and eastern Oregon are rocky and dry. The Snake River runs along the eastern border. It carves out a deep gorge called Hells Canyon.

Crater Lake is one of the top ten deepest lakes in the entire world.

FUN AT HELLS CANYON

Yahoo! You're bouncing past big rocks. And water's spraying all over you. You're rafting through Hells Canyon!

People love this area along the Snake River. They can hike or ride horses there, too.

Snowcapped Mount Hood is another favorite spot in Oregon. Many cities hold winter carnivals and skiing contests. Rodeos are also popular events.

You'll see sand dunes and rocky cliffs along the coast. Exploring the mountains is fun, too.

Hells Canyon has more than 900 miles (1,448 km) of trails to hike. Don't forget about camping and kayaking!

Matt Groening invented The Simpsons cartoons. He was born in Portland.

The Oregon Museum of Science and Industry in Portland has interactive scientific exhibits.

Let's raft awhile, then hike awhile. Let's do some fishing, too. We can cook the fish over a campfire!

PACIFIC OCEAN

WASHINGTON

• Cannon Beach

• Portland

Oregon City

Mount Hood

Pendleton

Snake River

Hells Canyon

IDAHO

Oregon's first library opened in Oregon City in 1842. It was a subscription library.

Pendleton holds the Pendleton Round-Up in September. It features a rodeo with an Old West theme.

Cannon Beach holds a sand castle contest every summer. People build cars, pigs, fish, and all kinds of things out of sand!

Hells Canyon is the country's deepest river gorge. It's deeper than Arizona's Grand Canyon.

9

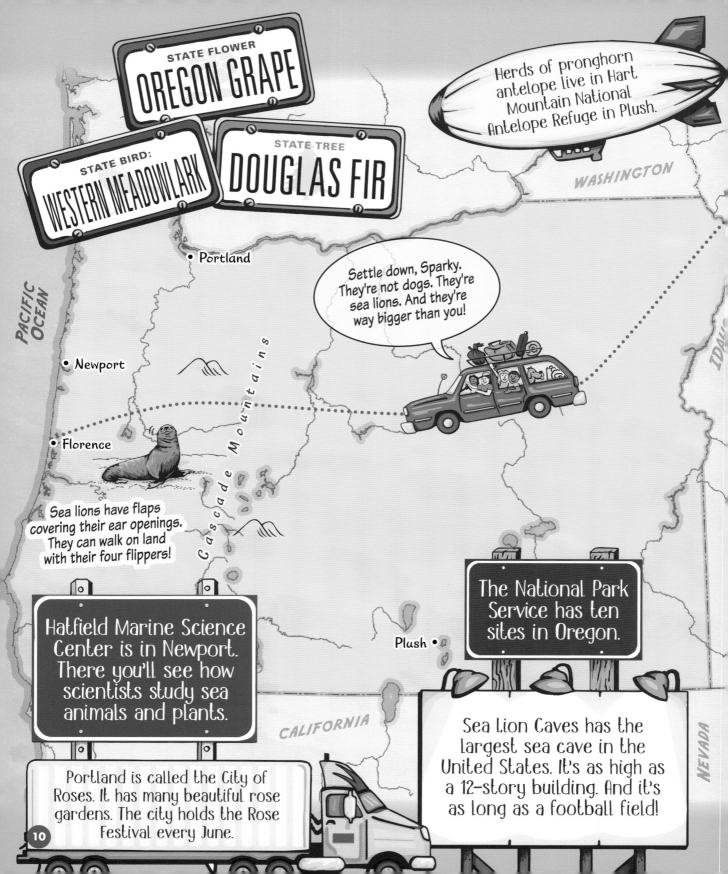

STATE FLOWER
OREGON GRAPE

STATE BIRD:
WESTERN MEADOWLARK

STATE TREE
DOUGLAS FIR

Herds of pronghorn antelope live in Hart Mountain National Antelope Refuge in Plush.

WASHINGTON

PACIFIC OCEAN

• Portland

Settle down, Sparky. They're not dogs. They're sea lions. And they're way bigger than you!

• Newport

Cascade Mountains

IDAHO

• Florence

Sea lions have flaps covering their ear openings. They can walk on land with their four flippers!

Plush •

The National Park Service has ten sites in Oregon.

Hatfield Marine Science Center is in Newport. There you'll see how scientists study sea animals and plants.

CALIFORNIA

NEVADA

Sea Lion Caves has the largest sea cave in the United States. It's as high as a 12-story building. And it's as long as a football field!

Portland is called the City of Roses. It has many beautiful rose gardens. The city holds the Rose Festival every June.

10

Head down to the rocky coast. Soon you'll hear a terrible racket. Is it barking dogs? Or roaring lions? Neither. It's sea lions!

You're visiting Sea Lion Caves near Florence. Approximately 200 sea lions live there. Some hang out in the cave. Others lounge on the rocks. And they all make lots of noise!

You'll spot many other animals along the coast. Sometimes giant whales are swimming offshore. People come from miles around to see them.

Deer, elk, and bighorn sheep live in the mountains. East of the Cascades, you'll find antelope. Almost half the state is forestland. Foxes, coyotes, and beavers make their homes there.

Sea lions love caves. Can you hear them barking?

THE MUSEUM AT WARM SPRINGS

Step inside a Native American **plank house**. See Native American masks, tools, baskets, and clothes. Hear tribal **elders** tell **traditional** tales. You're visiting the Museum at Warm Springs! It's on the Warm Springs **Reservation**. Three Native American groups live here. They are called the Confederated Tribes of Warm Springs. They were moved here from their homelands in 1885.

Years ago, these people found plentiful food in the forest. They dug for roots with special digging sticks. Deer and other large animals provided meat. Historically, the Chinook caught salmon in the Columbia River using long spears. Then they dried and stored the fish for winter.

The Confederated Tribes of the Warm Springs often celebrate with powwows.

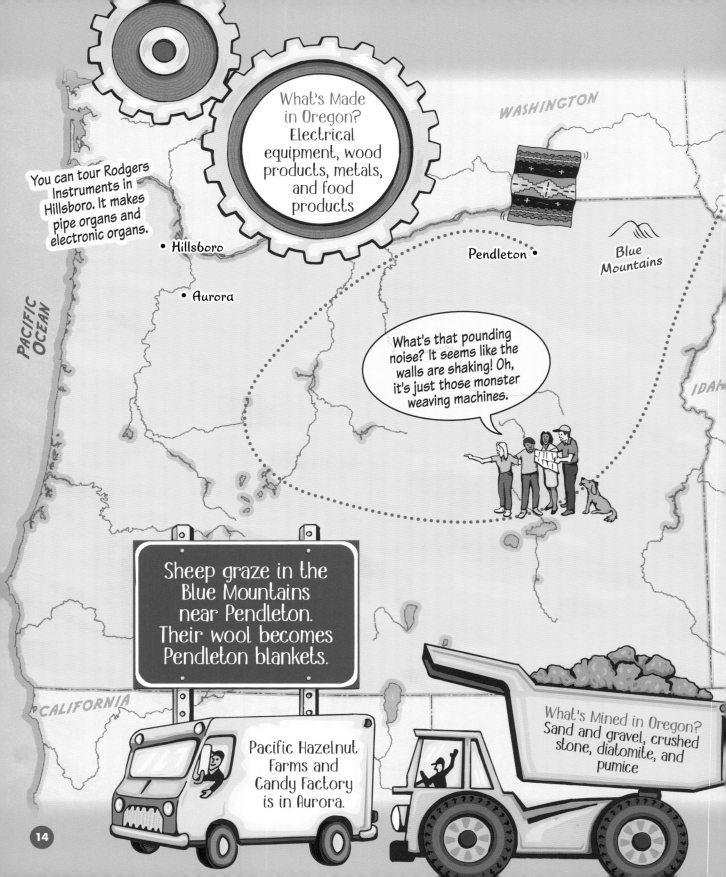

You can tour Rodgers Instruments in Hillsboro. It makes pipe organs and electronic organs.

What's Made in Oregon? Electrical equipment, wood products, metals, and food products

• Hillsboro

• Aurora

WASHINGTON

Pendleton •

Blue Mountains

IDAHO

PACIFIC OCEAN

What's that pounding noise? It seems like the walls are shaking! Oh, it's just those monster weaving machines.

Sheep graze in the Blue Mountains near Pendleton. Their wool becomes Pendleton blankets.

CALIFORNIA

Pacific Hazelnut Farms and Candy Factory is in Aurora.

What's Mined in Oregon? Sand and gravel, crushed stone, diatomite, and pumice

TOURING PENDLETON WOOLEN MILLS

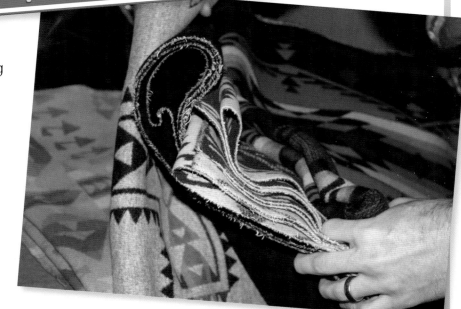

Here come big bundles of brightly colored wool. Spinning machines spin it into yarn. Then the yarn goes to the weaving room. The noisy looms weave it into rugs!

You're touring Pendleton Woolen Mills. Blankets are made here that have Native American–inspired designs.

Oregon's factories make all kinds of goods. Electronic equipment is the top factory product. That includes computer parts and calculators. Wood products are important, too. Forest trees are made into lumber, cardboard, and paper.

Pendleton Woolen Mills has made blankets since 1895.

FORT CLATSOP NEAR ASTORIA

Some people are carving logs into canoes. Others are making candles or smoking meat. Everyone's dressed like people from the 1800s. It's a living-history program at Fort Clatsop near Astoria!

Explorers camped here during the winter of 1805–1806. They were in a group with Meriwether Lewis and William Clark. These men had come west from Missouri. They were led by a Shoshone woman named Sacagawea. Sacagawea helped Lewis and Clark communicate with Native Americans along the way. They hoped to reach the Pacific Ocean. And they did! They followed the Columbia River to the ocean. They couldn't have done it without the help of Sacagawea.

Fur traders soon arrived in Oregon. They set up many trading posts. Missionaries settled in Oregon in 1834. Soon a flood of settlers poured in!

Lewis and Clark's team of explorers were called the Corps of Discovery.

Oregon was the 33rd state to enter the Union. It joined on February 14, 1859.

WASHINGTON

IDA

PACIFIC OCEAN

Oregon Trail

Oregon City

Willamette Valley

Kids along the Oregon Trail had lots of chores. They gathered wood for campfires, fetched buckets of water, and milked cows.

In 1877, the Nez Percé were ordered to a reservation. Refusing to be told where to live, Chief Joseph led a group of the Nez Percé to Canada. But he was forced to surrender near the Canadian border.

The Oregon Trail began in Independence, Missouri. Approximately 900 people took the trail to Oregon in 1843.

CALIFORNIA

The Oregon Trail was rough. It crossed mountains, rivers, and deserts. The trip along the entire trail took approximately six months.

Gold was discovered in eastern Oregon in 1860.

THE END OF THE OREGON TRAIL INTERPRETIVE CENTER

Check out the big covered wagons. Watch the **pioneers** work and cook. Walk along deep **ruts** in the ground. The wheels from real pioneers' wagons dug those ruts! You're visiting the End of the Oregon Trail Interpretive Center. It's in Oregon City. It explores life along the Oregon Trail.

Thousands of people headed west along that trail. They traveled it from the 1840s to the 1880s. They had heard about the Willamette Valley. They hoped to begin farming there.

Native Americans and settlers sometimes clashed. The Native Americans were being pushed off their homelands. Finally, the U.S. government forced them onto reservations.

Pioneers traveled across the country in wagons. Can you imagine doing that today?

THE STATE CAPITOL IN SALEM

See that statue atop the capitol? It glistens in the sunlight. It's the Golden Pioneer! This statue honors Oregon's early settlers. They had to be tough to survive! Then step inside the capitol. You'll see huge paintings of pioneer life.

The capitol is the center of state government. Oregon's government has three branches. The legislative assembly makes up one branch. Its members make the state's laws. You can even watch them at work. The governor leads another branch. This branch carries out the laws. The third branch applies the law to court cases. This branch is made up of judges.

This is Oregon's third capitol building. It was built in 1938.

The name Salem comes from the Hebrew word *shalom*, meaning "peace."

Let's go up to the Golden Pioneer! We only have to climb 121 steps. They circle round and round inside the tower.

WASHINGTON

PACIFIC OCEAN

• Oregon City

Salem ★

IDAHO

Oregon City was the first capital of Oregon Territory. Salem became the capital city in 1852.

Be sure to see the Moon Tree on the capitol grounds. It grew from a seed carried aboard the *Apollo 14* mission to the moon in 1971!

You can visit Mission Mill Village in Salem. It has historic houses and working mill equipment. Mills were early factories.

Welcome to Salem, the capital of Oregon!

Oregon's state motto is "she flies with her own wings."

In 2016, 4,093,465 people lived in Oregon. It's the 27th-largest state by population.

WASHINGTON

PACIFIC OCEAN

Portland

Salem

Willamette Valley

Let's check out the yo-yo demonstration! Let's watch the puppet show!

IDAHO

Eugene

Oregon's early pioneers settled in the Willamette Valley. That region still has Oregon's biggest cities.

Día de Nuestra Señora de Guadalupe is a **Hispanic** festival held in Medford every year. Approximately 1 in 12 Oregonians are Hispanic.

Medford

CALIFORNIA

The traditional Chinese calendar is a lunar calendar. That is, it's based on stages of the moon. Chinese New Year is on a different day every year. It's often in February.

Portland's Chinese New Year celebration lasts two weeks.

Population of Largest Cities

Portland	632,309
Eugene	163,460
Salem	164,549

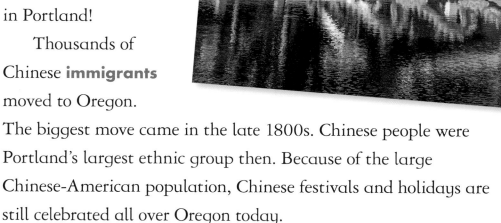

Snap, crackle, pop! Fireworks are exploding everywhere. And a giant dragon snakes down the street. It's Chinese New Year in Portland!

Thousands of Chinese **immigrants** moved to Oregon. The biggest move came in the late 1800s. Chinese people were Portland's largest ethnic group then. Because of the large Chinese-American population, Chinese festivals and holidays are still celebrated all over Oregon today.

Immigrants arrived from many other countries. Some came from Germany, England, or Ireland. Others came from Norway, Sweden, or Italy. They all made new homes in Oregon.

People decorate for Chinese New Year with dragons, which represent excellence in Chinese culture.

THE WILD HORSE ROUNDUP

Have you ever seen a wild horse? Just visit the Wild Horse **Corrals** near Burns. You'll see dozens of these beautiful animals there.

Thousands of wild horses roam around Oregon. Their **ancestors** escaped from settlers or miners. Sometimes the herds grow too big. There's not enough grass for them all. Then farmers ride out on the range. They round up lots of horses. Helicopters help with the roundup, too.

The horses are herded into holding pens. Next they're brought to the corral. Then some people are allowed to adopt a horse. They can give it lots of space and food.

However, some groups are against this practice. Groups such as the Humane Society of the United States think there are too many horses being held in captivity.

Did you know wild horses are actually a species of horse? Come see them at the Wild Horse Corrals!

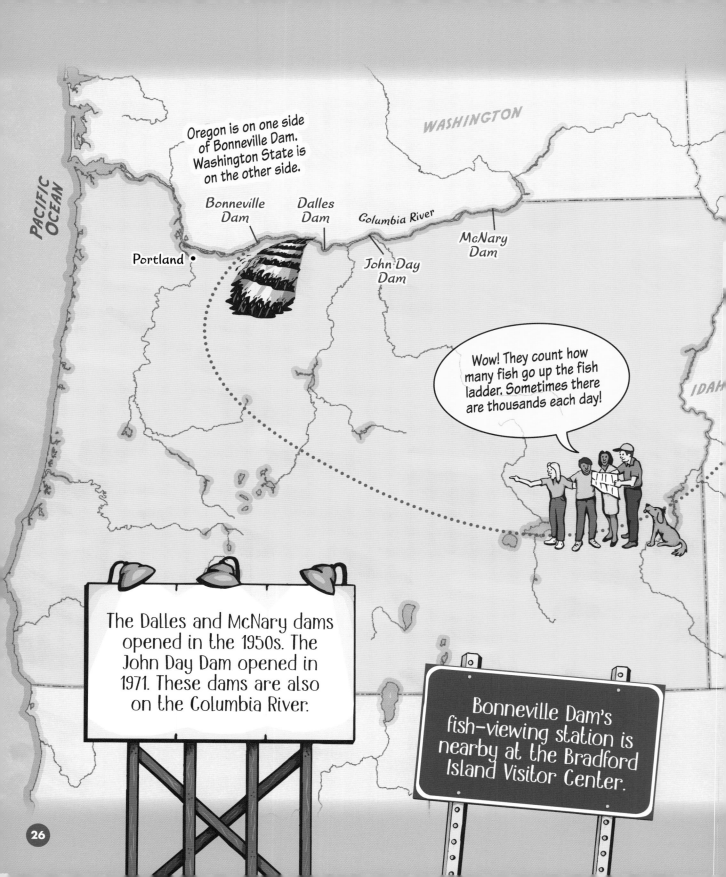

WASHINGTON

Oregon is on one side of Bonneville Dam. Washington State is on the other side.

Bonneville Dam

Dalles Dam

Columbia River

McNary Dam

John Day Dam

PACIFIC OCEAN

Portland

IDAHO

Wow! They count how many fish go up the fish ladder. Sometimes there are thousands each day!

The Dalles and McNary dams opened in the 1950s. The John Day Dam opened in 1971. These dams are also on the Columbia River.

Bonneville Dam's fish-viewing station is nearby at the Bradford Island Visitor Center.

FISH LADDERS AT BONNEVILLE DAM

Splash, splash! You're watching salmon jump up the fish ladder. You're at Bonneville Dam! This dam is on the Columbia River near Portland. It was built to create water-powered electricity. The dam created problems for salmon, though.

Salmon are born farther up the river. Then they swim down to the ocean. In time, they're ready to reproduce. They swim back upriver to do this. But the dam is in their way. That's why fish ladders were built. The ladders are like pools arranged in stair steps. The fish jump to higher and higher levels.

Bonneville Dam opened in 1938. Oregon built many more dams. A lot of them have fish ladders!

Have you ever seen a salmon jump? You will at Bonneville Dam!

STARGAZING ON PINE MOUNTAIN

Do you like staying up late? Then visit Pine Mountain **Observatory**! This stargazing center is near Bend. It sits high atop Pine Mountain.

The observatory has three massive telescopes. They let you see objects in the night sky. Sometimes the skies are extremely clear. Then people keep watching all night!

The University of Oregon owns this observatory. Scientists study the stars there. They might see black holes or exploding stars. Their discoveries are important. They help solve the mysteries of the universe.

Pine Mountain is located in the Deschutes National Forest. Take a look at that view!

TOURING TILLAMOOK CHEESE

Do you like grilled-cheese sandwiches? That cheese started out as milk. How did it turn into cheese? Just visit Tillamook Cheese. You'll see how it all happens!

First, workers cook the milk. It separates into **curds** and **whey**. They drain off the whey. Then they press the curds into blocks. Presto! Cheese!

Milk is an important farm product in Oregon. Farmers raise both dairy and beef cattle. Greenhouse and nursery plants are the top crops. Oregon is good at growing flowers from **bulbs**. Forest trees are leading products, too. Some of them end up as Christmas trees!

See how this cheese gets made when you tour the Tillamook Cheese factory. Maybe even take some home with you!

JOHN DAY FOSSIL BEDS

You see an enormous bone. It's bigger than your arm! It belonged to an early rhinoceros. It was found at John Day Fossil Beds National Monument.

This site is in northern Oregon. It spreads across a big area. You'll see the rhinoceros bone in the Thomas Condon Paleontology Center. It's in the visitor center near Dayville.

Many scientists work at the fossil beds. They dig up fossils there. Then they study them. They've found fossils of fish, birds, insects, and plants. They've found horses, saber-toothed cats, and sea tortoises. You can watch the scientists at work. Just drop by the museum!

The John Day Fossil Beds National Monument spans across 14,000 acres (5,666 ha).

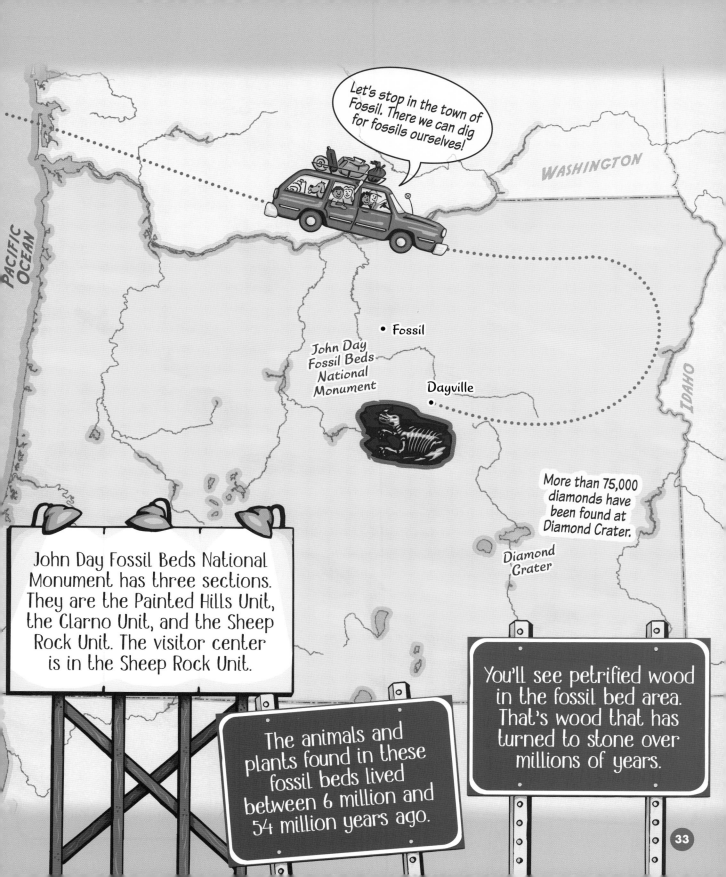

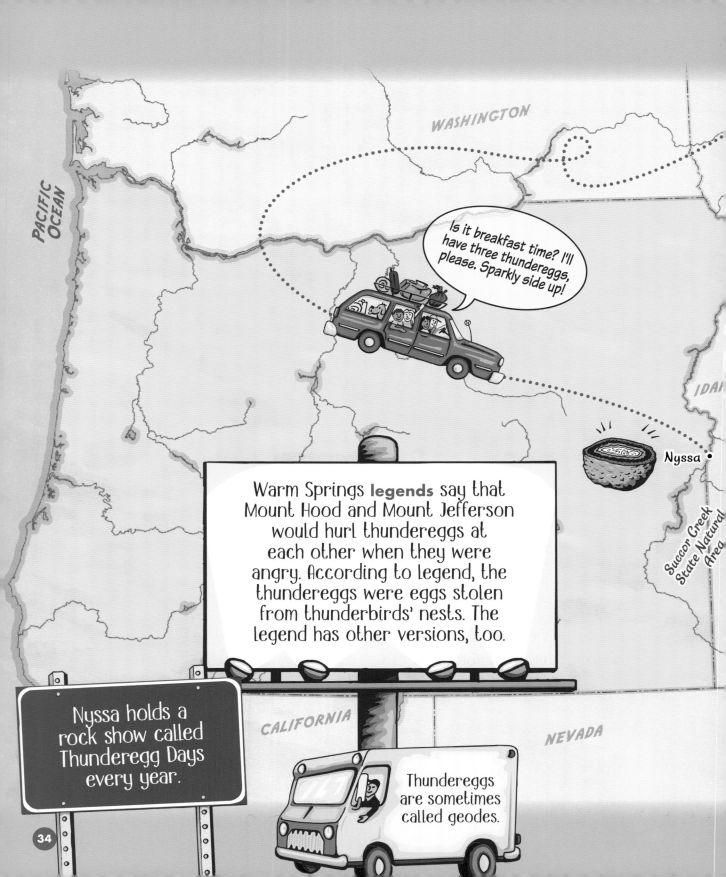

WASHINGTON

PACIFIC OCEAN

IDAH

Is it breakfast time? I'll have three thundereggs, please. Sparkly side up!

Nyssa

Succor Creek State Natural Area

Warm Springs **legends** say that Mount Hood and Mount Jefferson would hurl thundereggs at each other when they were angry. According to legend, the thundereggs were eggs stolen from thunderbirds' nests. The legend has other versions, too.

Nyssa holds a rock show called Thunderegg Days every year.

CALIFORNIA

NEVADA

Thundereggs are sometimes called geodes.

THUNDEREGGS AT SUCCOR CREEK

You've heard of thunderclouds. You've heard of thunderstorms. Maybe you've even heard of thunderbirds. But have you ever heard of thundereggs?

The thunderegg is Oregon's state rock. Thunder eggs don't look that great on the outside. They're just sort of lumpy and brown. But crack one open. The inside sparkles like colored glass!

You can hunt for thunder eggs at many sites. Succor Creek State Natural Area near Nyssa is a good spot. Some thunder eggs are as small as marbles. But others can weigh hundreds of pounds. Happy rock-hunting!

Most thundereggs are the size of a baseball. Check out the thunderegg collection at Succor Creek.

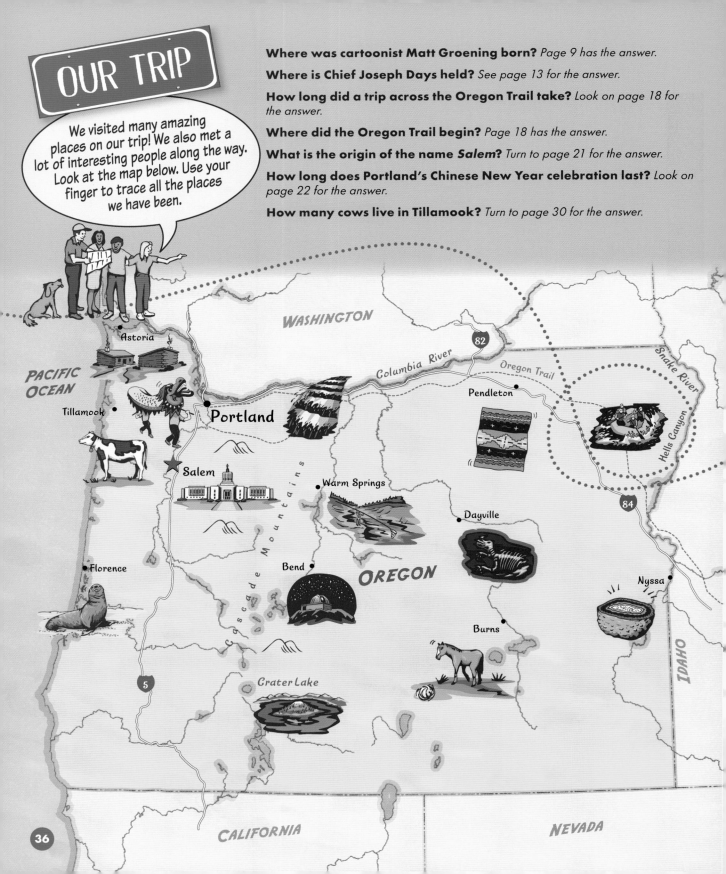

OUR TRIP

We visited many amazing places on our trip! We also met a lot of interesting people along the way. Look at the map below. Use your finger to trace all the places we have been.

Where was cartoonist Matt Groening born? *Page 9 has the answer.*

Where is Chief Joseph Days held? *See page 13 for the answer.*

How long did a trip across the Oregon Trail take? *Look on page 18 for the answer.*

Where did the Oregon Trail begin? *Page 18 has the answer.*

What is the origin of the name Salem? *Turn to page 21 for the answer.*

How long does Portland's Chinese New Year celebration last? *Look on page 22 for the answer.*

How many cows live in Tillamook? *Turn to page 30 for the answer.*

WASHINGTON

Astoria

PACIFIC OCEAN

Tillamook

Columbia River

Portland

Oregon Trail

Pendleton

Snake River

Hells Canyon

82

Salem

Warm Springs

Dayville

84

Florence

Bend

OREGON

Nyssa

Cascade Mountains

Burns

5

Crater Lake

IDAHO

CALIFORNIA

NEVADA

State flag

State seal

That was a great trip! We have traveled all over Oregon! There are a few places that we didn't have time for, though. Next time, we plan to visit the Portland Children's Museum. Kids can explore several hands-on exhibits. Visitors can enjoy everything from science activities to live performances!

STATE SYMBOLS

State animal: American beaver

State beverage: Milk

State bird: Western meadowlark

State dance: Square dance

State fish: Chinook salmon

State flower: Oregon grape

State gemstone: Oregon sunstone

State insect: Oregon swallowtail butterfly

State mushroom: Pacific golden chanterelle

State nut: Hazelnut

State rock: Thunderegg (geode)

State seashell: Oregon hairy triton (conch)

State tree: Douglas fir

STATE SONG

"OREGON, MY OREGON"

Words by J. A. Buchanan, music by Henry B. Murtagh

Land of the Empire Builders,
Land of the Golden West;
Conquered and held by free men,
Fairest and the best.
Onward and upward ever,
Forward and on, and on;
Hail to thee, Land of Heroes,
My Oregon.

Land of the rose and sunshine,
Land of the summer's breeze;
Laden with health and vigor,
Fresh from the Western seas.
Blest by the blood of martyrs,
Land of the setting sun;

Hail to thee, Land of Promise,
My Oregon.

FAMOUS PEOPLE

Beard, James (1903–1985), chef and author

Burrell, Ty (1967–), actor

Cleary, Beverly (1916–), children's book author

Duniway, Abigail Jane Scott (1834–1915), leader of the women's rights movement in Oregon

Groening, Matt (1954–), cartoonist and creator of *The Simpsons*

Hatfield, Mark O. (1922–2011), politician

Joseph, Chief (ca. 1840–1904), Nez Percé leader

Kingman, Dave (1948–), former baseball player

Le Guin, Ursula K. (1929–), author

Markham, Edwin (1852–1940), poet

McGinley, Phyllis (1905–1978), poet and author

McLoughlin, John (1784–1857), fur trader who helped settle Oregon

Miller, Joaquin (1837–1913), poet

Pauling, Linus (1901–1994), chemist and Nobel Prize winner

Prefontaine, Steve (1951–1975), Olympic runner

Rashad, Ahmad (1949–), sportscaster and former football player

Reed, John (1887–1920), journalist

Schroeder, Patricia Scott (1940–), former politician

Simon, Norton (1907–1993), industrialist and art collector

WORDS TO KNOW

ancestors (AN-sess-turz) parents, grandparents, great-grandparents, and so on

bulbs (BUHLBZ) underground buds from which some plants grow

corrals (kor-ALZ) fenced pens where livestock are kept

curds (KURDZ) lumps formed when milk is thickened by heating or age

elders (ELL-durz) older people respected for being wise

fossils (FOSS-uhlz) prints or remains of plants or animals found in rock

Hispanic (hiss-PAN-ik) having roots in Spanish-speaking lands

immigrants (IM-uh-gruhnts) people who move from their homeland to another country

legends (LEJ-undz) imaginary tales handed down from earlier times

observatory (uhb-ZUR-vuh-tor-ee) a building set up for watching stars and distant objects

pioneers (pie-uh-NEERZ) the first people to explore or settle in an unknown land

plank house (PLANK HOWSS) a long log house built by certain northwestern Native Americans

reservation (rez-ur-VAY-shuhn) a piece of land set aside for special use, such as for Native Americans

ruts (RUHTS) deep grooves or ditches

traditional (truh-DISH-uh-nuhl) following long-held customs

whey (HWAY) the watery part of milk that separates from the curds

TO LEARN MORE

IN THE LIBRARY

Cohen, Fiona. *Curious Kids Nature Guide: Explore the Amazing Outdoors of the Pacific Northwest*. Seattle, WA: Little Bigfoot, 2017.

Felix, Rebecca. *What's Great about Oregon?* Minneapolis, MN: Lerner, 2015.

Gregory, Josh. *If You Were a Kid on the Oregon Trail*. New York, NY: Scholastic, 2017.

ON THE WEB

Visit our Web site for links about Oregon:
childsworld.com/links

Note to Parents, Teachers, and Librarians: We routinely verify our Web links to make sure they are safe and active sites. So encourage your readers to check them out!

PLACES TO VISIT OR CONTACT

Oregon Historical Society
ohs.org
1200 SW Park Avenue
Portland, OR 97205
503/222-1741
For more information about the history of Oregon

Oregon Tourism Commission
traveloregon.com
250 Church Street SE
Suite 100
Salem, OR 97301
503/967-1560
For more information about traveling in Oregon

Oregon covers 98,379 square miles (254,799 sq km). It's the 9th-largest state in size.

INDEX

Bye, Beaver State! We had a great time. We'll come back soon!